Dear Parent:

Clifford is so lucky! He has the unc[onditional love of]
Emily Elizabeth, the love every chil[d longs]
for. Emily Elizabeth is truly kind. S[he loves him]
when he is so small that some call [him a runt, and]
when he is so big that he can't fit through the door.
Whatever Clifford needs, she provides: first the food to help
him grow, and then an island to roam when no ordinary
house can contain him.

Emily Elizabeth's love and kindness help Clifford thrive. It
doesn't matter to her if he's big or small—and that may be
very meaningful to many young children who are concerned
about their own size. Think about the way it must feel to be
down there looking up, about how much they want to be big,
tall, and strong. They play out fantasies of being powerful and
important in order to escape feeling powerless in our big
adult-run world. Think about the fact that they don't get to
make a lot of decisions. When there is something they want
or want to do, they're often told, "No, not now. Maybe when
you're bigger." So when Clifford is too small to drink out of
his own water bowl, they can understand his plight. But then
when he gets so big that his size causes him trouble, they
are confronted by a new idea—that bigness may not be
everything.

So Clifford is a very lucky dog; for big or small,
he is important to Emily Elizabeth. She understands
what he needs and sees that he gets it. Whatever his
real size is, her kindness makes him feel just right.
And doing that for someone is very, very nice.

Adele M. Brodkin, Ph.D.

Visit Clifford at scholastic.com/clifford

ISBN 0-439-41192-0

Library of Congress Cataloging-in-Publication Data is available

10 9 8 7 6 5 4 3   01 02 03 04 05 06

Printed in the U.S.A.   24
First printing, February 2001

Clifford THE BIG RED DOG®

A Puppy to Love

Adapted by Bob Barkly

Illustrated by John Kurtz

**Based on the Scholastic books
Clifford the Small Red Puppy
and Clifford's Puppy Days
by Norman Bridwell**

From the television script
"Little Clifford" by Baz Hawkins

Cartwheel
·B·O·O·K·S·®

SCHOLASTIC INC.

New York   Toronto   London   Auckland   Sydney   Mexico City
New Delhi   Hong Kong

Each year on my birthday,
I made the same wish:
Not for a kitten
And not for a fish,
Not for a bunny,
A hamster, or dove.
What did I wish for?
A puppy to love.

And one happy day,

My wishes came true.

My folks cried, "Surprise!

We have good news for you."

The dog next door had puppies.

Not one, not two, but three.

Our neighbor, Mr. Bradley, said,

"There's one for Emily."

"Take your pick," he told me.

"Which one do you choose?

They're all so cute," he added.

"There's no way you can lose."

I looked at Puppy Number One.

I looked at Puppy Two.

But Puppy Three

Was made for me.

No other pup would do.

"The dog's a runt,"
My parents warned.
"He always will be small."
"That's okay," I told them.
"He needs me most of all."

The little red puppy
Plopped down in my hat.
He gave me a slurp,
And that was that!

"Let's call him Tiny,"
Mommy said.
My dad suggested Red.
But to me he looked
Like a Clifford.
I named him that instead.

We walked to the pet shop
To buy some supplies.
Daddy gave me a dollar
To buy Clifford a collar . . .

But they didn't have one his size.

Back home we lost Clifford

Again and again.

He hid in Dad's slipper;
We found him, but then . . .

He stood on two legs
To drink from his bowl.

He lost his balance.

He started to roll
Around in the water . . .
Around and around.

Poor little Clifford—
He almost drowned!

I fed him and loved him.

It didn't take long

Till my little red puppy

Grew healthy and strong.

Clifford grew from the bottom.

He grew from the top.

He grew and he grew.

He just wouldn't stop!

He grew and he grew

And he grew some more. . . .

Uh-oh, Clifford!

Watch out for that door!

"Tsk! Tsk!" said my mother.
"It's really a pity.
Our big red dog, Clifford,
Has outgrown the city.
We'll have to find
Another home
With lots of space
For him to roam."

So we loaded Clifford onto a truck
And drove down to the pier.

I can't say it was easy,

But we finally made it here.

Now we live on an island

In the middle of the sea,

Where there's lots of room

To run and play

For Clifford and for me.

BOOKS IN THIS SERIES:

Welcome to Birdwell Island: Everyone on Birdwell Island thinks that Clifford is just too big! But when there's an emergency, Clifford The Big Red Dog teaches everyone to have respect—even for those who are different.

A Puppy to Love: Emily Elizabeth's birthday wish comes true: She gets a puppy to love! And with her love and kindness, Clifford The Small Red Puppy becomes Clifford The Big Red Dog!

The Big Sleep Over: Clifford has to spend his first night without Emily Elizabeth. When he has trouble falling asleep, his Birdwell Island friends work together to make sure that he—and everyone else—gets a good night's sleep.

No Dogs Allowed: No dogs in Birdwell Island Park? That's what Mr. Bleakman says—before he realizes that sharing the park with dogs is much more fun.

An Itchy Day: Clifford has an itchy patch! He's afraid to go to the vet, so he tries to hide his scratching from Emily Elizabeth. But Clifford soon realizes that it's better to be truthful and trust the person he loves most— Emily Elizabeth.

The Doggy Detectives: Oh, no! Emily Elizabeth is accused of stealing Jetta's gold medal—and then her shiny mirror! But her dear Clifford never doubts her innocence and, with his fellow doggy detectives, finds the real thief.

Follow the Leader: While playing follow-the-leader with Clifford and T-Bone, Cleo learns that playing fair is the best way to play!

The Big Red Mess: Clifford tries to stay clean for the Dog of the Year contest, but he ends up becoming a big red mess! However, when Clifford helps the judge reach the shore safely, he finds that he doesn't need to stay clean to be the Dog of the Year.

The Big Surprise: Poor Clifford. It's his birthday, but none of his friends will play with him. Maybe it's because they're all busy . . . planning his surprise party!

The Wild Ice Cream Machine: Charley and Emily Elizabeth decide to work the ice cream machine themselves. Things go smoothly . . . until the lever gets stuck and they find themselves knee-deep in ice cream!

Dogs and Cats: Can dogs and cats be friends? Clifford, T-Bone, and Cleo don't think so. But they have a change of heart after they help two lost kittens find their mother.

The Magic Ball: Emily Elizabeth trusts Clifford to deliver a package to the post office, but he opens it and breaks the gift inside. Clifford tries to hide his blunder, but Emily Elizabeth appreciates honesty and understands that accidents happen.